Letters to my *Lover*

MAVEN PRESS

 A catalogue record for this
work is available from the
National Library of Australia

NATIONAL
LIBRARY
OF AUSTRALIA

National Library of Australia Catalogue-in-Publication data:
Letters to my Lover/Laura Elizabeth

ISBN: 978-0-6456356-6-9
(Print)
ISBN: 978-0-6456356-5-2
(Ebook)

Acknowledgements

In unity, we honour and pay our respects to the custodians of Whadjuk Noongar Boodjar country, the lands on which this book was first seeded.

We pay our respects to the Elders both past and present
and to those emerging.
The stories within these pages may contain sensitive content and/or
memories of loved ones who have passed on,
which may activate a response within you.

Please read with awareness and care.

Lisa Bito

Renaissance

Dear Lover,

This is a tribute to the journey of loving myself—the dawning of the new me.

The knowledge I need to finish my *Letter to my Lover* makes me feel sick. The journey to self-love is a roller-coaster. Words written months ago now don't feel right. I'm on the roller-coaster's downward slide, knowing the upward thrill will come, but I feel nauseous at the concept of fully sitting in, loving and accepting me. Honesty with you, the reader, seems important for the reason a glint of recognition might come your way. There is no upward thrill without the corresponding slide downward, and it feels important to acknowledge this. If realisation is your takeaway from my words, then my job is done.

So, to my words from months before …

A renaissance occurs within—a stirring deep in my soul, womb space, and heart. A homecoming. It's a strange thing called self-love. Strange to me, at least. A concept that was unknown to me four years ago. Foreign land never traversed before. A desert never crossed. The unknown, wild woods never explored. The path never travelled. Virgin territory, unblemished by any mark or footprints. Barren land, a place of nothing except dry aridness.

You get the idea, I'm sure!

The renaissance began in a hall in Upwey. A place of community, a place of loving support among a circle of women forever imprinted on my heart. It was a time in the week that I was alone, which was a huge deal for me. A turbulent household, a demanding job and three children to care for and play mum taxi service meant no time for *me*.

It was a game changer, this place and space that began to replenish my soul. Unknown at first, but a time and a place I was never willing to give up. I still carve out a space in the week. The place to start the long journey back to worth and self-love. Those feelings had always existed deep within me but had never been acknowledged or accepted. Feelings that exist within everybody, recognised or not—feelings I can now freely claim as my own.

They exist in a place of homage, a place of sacred space, my temple, which I visit frequently and lovingly. I sit in a space where I can freely declare to myself, *I love you. You're an amazing human being, and I love you.* Saying these words has become easier, but meaning them deep in my heart and soul every time I declare them, as I now can, is hard.

Some days it's still a battle, some days, it's a victory, but it's a declaration that starts every one of my days. Saying those words aloud or within and feeling them flooding my heart space is a wondrous, exhilarating, no place on earth like it feeling. And I revel in it!

There are days when the words don't stir my heart, but I now know that they'll always return. So, I choose to say them anyway, every day, in celebration of me and the road I've travelled. A state of bliss welcomed with exultation on the good days, a state of blah and no meaning on the other days, but they spill from my mouth and into my mind anyway. It's now an ingrained habit and how I begin my day.

Notice the word *choose*, it is important! It's telling me I'm important, worthy and loved by myself. And that is the only person who matters in the end.

The old version of me used to scatter pieces of myself deliberately to make sure everything and everyone was covered. Part of this journey back to love has been deliberately taking back those golden pieces of me strewn everywhere to reunite me to a shining treasure sparkling with magnificence, worth, and self-love.

Learning to be vulnerable is okay. Learning that my heart breaking open again and again is okay. Speaking from my heart is okay. Speaking my truth is okay. Reclaiming my voice is okay. Dancing with fear and doing it anyway is okay. That's the journey of self-love and self-worth.

The path to enlightenment is through pain and your willingness to sit with it. So too, is the path to self-love. A willingness to face your pain and shadow. It's a path familiar to me—its contours, bends, and ups and downs, a well-trodden path. Not long and straight but meandering with unexpected twists and turns and unexpected spectacular vistas. A journey of spiralling inward and then back outward, a never-ending dance for eternity. A hard journey but the end rewards far outweigh the heartache on the way.

We come from love, and we end by going back to love. And the biggest rewards in life come from learning to love yourself.

My mantra to you is to acknowledge your magnificence: I love you, you flawed, imperfect, wondrous person. I love you wholeheartedly.

Every day you say that to yourself is a victory, no matter how small.

Milly Taylor

The Truest Love

Dear Lover,

I called for you in moon cycles and runes. Through the blood of Ancient Celts and Raven Goddess flight, on an altar of lavender and thyme. I sang you to me on a river of love that I drifted on with you in every life. I do not know how to half-love or hide my longing when it yearns for you. I feel like a blinding sun.

I do not hold my cards close to my chest or wear 'thick skin'. I cannot squeeze myself into a small box of detachment to appease others. It feels like a cage to a soul like mine. It makes me pace. It makes me plan my escape. It makes me wild.

Wild animals thrive when they run free. So, do not bind me to your trepidation of tenderness. We are all scared, but we can choose the things for which we are brave. Sometimes we fear the wrong things. Sometimes we fear what we desire most. Sometimes we fear the very things that are destined to liberate us.

Why dip mere toes into an ocean when we can immerse fully into cool waters and swim in a love that will replenish our soul first?

I am a lover. And every time I sense a wavering whisper call for me to quiet my soul to cater to a fear of love, I am shackled, and I rage through the chains with love-stained venom.

I will break those binds every time and leave you craving.

I would rather be sovereign in the forest than tethered to a stake in a barren wasteland. I will not stay where we cannot flourish. I will not give where we cannot overflow.

The more I am told to hold back, the more I want to run free, salivating and tearing the fresh ground with wild claws, freedom in my lungs, love in my bones, and you by my side.

My heart beats for love.
My blood runs for love.
This skin.
These eyes.
This body.
It's all love.

I am a rebel with an open heart. A wild, fucking beast that will love you harder than any walls you build. Try me. I will come for you every time and show you that true freedom is found, not in fear or hesitation, but in love and love alone. This is an invitation.

Tell me of your shadows and light.
I love the way it all dances on your skin.
Wild ones love deep.
If you are not ready for devotion to the waters,
stay within your walls.
I am in the currents with or without you.
I once rose from the ashes,
and walked into the forest.
I will not return to restraint for anyone.
To love a wild one, to be a wild one,
you must unveil your soul.

Willingly,
whole-heartedly.
Swallow the illusion of terror and find it is nothing but faithless-
ness.
The nourishment you seek is found amongst the daring.
Surrender to the path before you.
Remove your cloaks
and bare your chest to the sun.
I will run rivers to lead you home to your own heart,
and as souls touched by ecstasy entwine in moonlight.

The dirt beneath our bodies will seep into the weariness and bring us back to life.

You will find your bones have told the story that the wild is in your veins too.

You will find that love was calling you home to yourself all along.

You just needed to exhale to the wind to hear its song on the tip of your tongue.

The truest love shows you how to love yourself.

Love, Milly.

Rachel Carmichael

A Poem for my Lover

Dazed and delighted,
I lay, sticky-sweet, writing a letter to my lover.
I can barely lift pen to paper,
my body blissfully spent and my mind lost in its awe of you.

My hands distracted, I trace delicate spirals along your spine, and my
muscles contract as you quiver beneath my touch.
The room is thick with us.
Echoes of our moans haunt the fading light, and milky skin becomes
a tangled mess on satin sheets.

You've said it before, time melts away in these moments.
Every inch of you invites me to worship, and I oblige, dripping with
enthusiasm and wonder.
Devout is our practice.
We hold each other sovereign to the world beyond our gasps and
sighs.

My only thought is your next touch.
The next taste.
The next tantalising brush of your breath on my skin before you lose yourself in me.
My fingers beckon you to surrender.
One, then two coaxing you towards breathless abandon.

We retire euphoric, but only for a moment.
It only takes one look, one kiss, one lingering lip, and the passion erupts again.
My pen and journal beckon me to write,
a letter to my lover.
To you …

But I've written every word across your skin with my mouth.

And now there are no words left to say …

Jessica Wright

The Fall

The girl you fell in love with was fierce. She was determined to rewrite her story and redefine herself. She was eager and passionate. She was driven and set to achieve greatness.

Then she met you. Don't panic! She was still this person. That's why you fell in love with her. Her outspokenness. Her will to correct the wrong in the world. But she had fears, ones that were ingrained deeply within her soul. Trauma that loomed around childhood, feelings of being let down, neglected, and feelings of disappointment, were the only ones she was familiar with.

This is me—your love.

If I knew one thing, it was that I couldn't feel any of those again. The deep-rooted belief that I was too much. Unlovable and that everyone would end up hurting me, eventually. Because if I were to identify a pattern in my life, that would be it. For so long, this passage of thought was holding me hostage.

You were all in, and I was too. But for the prologue of our love story, I wouldn't let you touch me. And when you did, I cried. I didn't cry because you hurt me. Not because I was scared. But because when you did, it was pure love. And I had never felt that kind of touch before.

The intimate touch of someone who saw my raw soul and loved it, didn't wish to change it, quiet it or run away from it, was pure acceptance. I felt that for the first time. You wanted me, and God, I wanted you. Fear couldn't hold me back from you.

I knew you were the one—my person. But I didn't know how I was supposed to overcome this need to run. I felt like I'd been deprived of the most natural feeling you encounter within our human experience. But now, after being starved of love or only shown the bare minimum of a healthy relationship, I had the most divine experience standing right in front of me, and I had to let myself fall.

Luckily, you caught me.

We fell fast. Every second was spent by each other's side. Well, in reality, we were attached at the hip every second. We didn't have the responsibilities of being a working adult. In the moments we were apart, we were yearning for each other like the love-struck souls we were.

Fast forward to when I fell in love with you all over again. One thousand times harder! The birth of our son. The birth of a new love. One so deep that it would kill you if it wasn't love.

You held me as I birthed our son. The biggest moment in our collective lives. Where life as we knew it changed, and we met the most angelic, tiny human. Our Son. Half of me and half of you. Conception, pregnancy, and childbirth blow my mind even more after going through them.

We made a human. He was in a rush to be created. Making his presence known early within our grand love story. Our biggest blessing, our best friend. There was no stopping him. He was made with pure love. The textbook fireworks between lovers, kind of love. A love that lets go of fear. A love that completely surrendered and embraced the path we had embarked on together. United spiritually, emotionally, and physically. Our genetic materials chose each other, and the most wonderful creation came from that.

I love you.

I have loved you from the moment I laid my eyes on you. That deep, wild, powerful connection entwined our souls together. Who was I kidding when we first met? I couldn't resist you. I couldn't have let my fear consume me again. Not this time, and never again.

Thank you, my love.

For being my lover. For teaching me what touch feels like when it's driven by love. By a sincere want for nothing but eternal devotion. For the goosebumps. The kisses that send surges of little fireworks through each and every nerve in my body.

Thank you for your moments of fire. For when the determined, fierce woman in me needed to retreat, you protected me. You held me and scared the scary away.

Tears of joy fall down my cheek as I think of our love. In the simple knowing, that this is it. I am home.

Nathalie Biviano

Al Mio Amore

Zucchero Bello Mio,

Your humour magnetised me.

Your self-assurance hooked me.

Your integrity sealed the deal.

Seventeen years ago, you took me on that magic carpet ride and showed me a whole new world. You adored, cherished, and marvelled at me. You made me feel like the luckiest girl. I was your everything—I knew and felt every millimetre!

The love notes, the snacks packed, the helicopter, boating and bike rides, the dinners, the weekends away. You supported my overseas sojourn. You helped my parents when they lost the family home even when I wasn't in the country, being the solid presence when my brother was in the hospital. I'll never forget what this all imprinted: This guy is solid. He bloody loves me.

After our first juju bear, the real tests emerged. The mothering experience made me feel so invisible. Losing my father made me wobbly. Our connection felt like it had evaporated. And I wasn't prepared to accept this.

I wanted more.

More partnership.

A deeper conversation.

More passion.

More aspirational modelling for our kids.

More than mediocre.

I was aching to relate to you better and read every marriage book. We became so much better. After our second juju bear, we left Sydney to start fresh on the Gold Coast, just the four of us. Adventures ahead! I completely understood you had to provide for us. And it also felt really lonely when you weren't around.

I grappled insanely with being at home with the babies. It was so hard. I was so lost.

I didn't have anyone around. It was just you and me. And, unknowingly, I gave you jobs you never signed up for! When you didn't emotionally support me the way I needed you to, it hurt me, resentful, and so frustrated. I know better now—it's not your job to make me happy. It's mine.

I lacked the maturity to realise you didn't have the skills or bandwidth to support me in the way I needed. I just didn't know. That left me feeling I was no longer important to you. It felt like you'd given up on me and weren't nurturing me like before. In those moments, my inner world and heart collapsed. I pined for your solid presence. It was so hard.

Things weren't bad between us. I just struggled internally, trying to understand why I felt like such a failure. And you didn't know how to support me. It created judgement.

Your minimal communication style, coupled with my excessive one, tripped us up. I judged you for not being someone you weren't. Now I realise how unfair that was. I'm so sorry for judging you that way.

I dived deeper into books, podcasts and courses.

Matrescence. Masculine and feminine energies. Attachment theory. Nervous system work. Trauma responses. Polyvagal theory.

I know these terms slide like Teflon for you, but to my geeky mind, they've been the missing pieces! My mentors showed me what Disney never did. The lights turned on, and I was excited our love would accelerate and ascend.

I've learnt our personal growth looks different. Just because you have no idea who Deepak Chopra is, doesn't mean you aren't interested in evolving. In your own way, you've always remained grounded, which I'm so grateful for. It meant you were so stable in holding me through all my shifts and transformations.

Amongst all the teachers I've had, you've been my greatest. You watched me spiral, explore, rise, fall, and emotionally dance, and you never, ever once tried to change who I was or who I was becoming. Instead, you just let me be.

Thank you for this epic gift of true, unconditional acceptance.

I can now see our tensions stemmed from me urging you to be more like me. Your resistance taught me I need to truly accept you the way you've accepted me.

Thank you for this gift, Amore.

From all my inner healing, the biggest realisation is this: Hurt occurs in relationships because we make it mean something about ourselves. For example, he's not on board. Therefore, I am not important enough to him. In other words, we personalise other people's pain.

When I realised this, our relationship changed. I mean, really changed.

I stopped making it about me because I know I am worthy, important and enough.

When you disengage, it is because of your own pain from your historical wounds. It's nothing to do with not loving me.

It took me a long time to figure this out. And now I understand.

My rational brain 'gets it'. But I am human, after all. My involuntary emotions take over sometimes.

You see this when I retreat, bite, and am short fused.

It's because I'm afraid.

Afraid I won't be the most important thing in your life.

Afraid you'll not look at me the same.

Afraid our love, care and devotion for each other evaporates.

Afraid our individuation makes us too individual and leaves us incompatible.

Afraid that we 'miss' each other because we're unwilling to understand each other.

Afraid I'd have to accept what is and not be fully satisfied in this state.

Afraid that expressing my dissatisfaction is met with 'there's the front door', which means you're too closed off from even trying for our marriage.

Afraid that I'm too dependent on you to make me feel important.

Afraid that I can't adequately meet my own needs in that way, and then if I do, what do I need you for?

Yes, I can be afraid.

And, yes, I also hold certainty.

I am certain we will always find a way back to each other because we always do.

You're my home, my safety, my heart.

I love you more than you know, and I am so grateful you chose me.

Rachael Sarah

Billet-Doux

Under a canvas of blue sky, she runs across the grass-green school grounds, spindly legs darting forward, light as air can be. There he is, standing under the old Tick-Tock Tree—waiting to be picked up from school for the last time.

The sprawling oval shortens, and she nears him. Warm rays of the summer sun on fourteen-year-old skin, faint streaks of Vegemite on a pale blue summer dress. It's December, and the cicadas click and whirl, fading amidst her roaring heartbeat.

The light scent of lemon gum lifts the air and mingles with that certain type of magic—first-love magic. She had felt it before. The reminder catches her breath, stopping her in her tracks. She remembered the tumble of golden waves against his freckled forehead, the glimmer in his eyes, the tilt of his head, and the way his hand had brushed over hers.

She wipes sweaty palms down the smooth fabric of her dress and imagines the next part over and over. Sometimes she reaches him, unable to offer anything more than a simple goodbye. Other times she makes it across the lawn only to turn back because her mind struggles against the age-old question, *What if?*

Her favourite make-believe scenario is when she steps out of the shady gum trees and into the dewy afternoon light. Hopeful, she walks to him, their eyes meet, and on tiptoes, she kisses him on the cheek, a cheek smattered with freckles.

Reality is far less cinematic. One hurried look at the crowd of classmates that have formed around him means bold gestures lose the battle against the weight of uncertainty. Feet pooling in clouds of fog, brown school shoes weighed down as though they were cement. She settles into the afternoon shadows and looks on. She sees him, the boy she's known and maybe even loved in that fourteen-year-old kind of way, from a distance.

Tick. One year. Tock. Two years. Tick-Tock.

Three years of make-believe scenarios with time bending and folding, warping this way and that. She again looks on from a distance. This time, when his warm eyes turn to hers, she manages a restrained wave. Then he leaves, just like he did back then.

Tick-Tock.

A decade later, she is doing the unthinkable. The unimaginable. And most definitely, the inevitable. Because, you see, she's that girl. She's the girl on a December day, the girl that runs headlong toward him.

Salty air sways her pale cotton summer dress—not Vegemite streaked, not uniform shop-issued blue. This year, passers-by can feel it—the palpable openness of her heart, the pull upwards of buoyancy. Next to the red box, she holds a billet-doux in hand—a sweet letter brimming with words that echo a past December day.

She catches a glimpse of the first line. I believe in quarks and quasars and fulfilling the unfulfilled moments between these. And I just couldn't let the Earth tilt on its axis one more time without setting one of my own truths free. Then she seals the envelope.

It's almost like a dream. It happens so quickly. She presses the envelope to her chest, her heart, wondering if her words will change her world forever. Then, she feels the stiff card slipping away as she opens the rusted red hatch.

And it's gone in a flash. The dull thump of another story hits the bottom of the red, vibrating through her world and his.

Her fourteen-year-old self races ahead and becomes something she can track online. With every heartbeat, her words, her truth, travel from one state border to another and then another. And finally… delivered.

Tick. One day. Tock. Two days. Tick. Four days. Tock. Eight days. Tick-Tock. Tick-Tock. Tick-Tock. Thirty days later, the silence is deafening. Tickkkkkkkkk.

Tock. Seventy-five days later, she receives a reply. It's icy and dispassionate and seems to bring with it the harsh winds of winter. Of all the imagined scenarios, in the light of day, she didn't quite picture this one.

It takes her many moments to realise that when you go searching for the right one, he's always the wrong one. Those who go searching never find love. They find lovelessness in the form of boys who answer heartfelt letters with drab and dreary 'Kind regards'.

You see, back then, she hadn't known that people are not always meant to last forever in each other's lives. She hadn't known that ever so slowly the seasons change, the Earth tilts on its axis, and the people we once knew and loved fade into the shadows.

When she stood next to that little-red box, holding that letter, she hadn't known that the man who would embrace a love letter like that would surely find her.

Rebecca Lee

Poems for My Love

Desert of my Heart Space

It's a dusty place, dry and barren. The desert of my heart space.

What should be a flourishing oasis no longer thrives. Lush green is but a memory.

I wander barefoot on the heat-ridden sand. Stumbling upon prickly weeds. They pierce my skin and produce pain.

Mouth is parched, lips are cracked. The heat is getting to me.

I am desperate for water. A tide would flood me. Just small droplets, please, for sustenance and return of life.

I am desperate for shade. Not that of tin. A woven hessian, allowing the light to filter.

I am desperate for the sunset. A gentle change that offers soothing.

I must rest now beneath the glazing sun. There is no walk left within.

Bring me the water.

Bring me the shade.

Deliver me a sunset.

I will Take a Lover

Seamlessly interwoven
the depths in space and time

I will take a lover
allow the brokenness to shine

Overfilling the cup
being generous to the pour

A hay-haven love nest
I beat myself no more

Naked to the touch
tracing lines under her skin

I will take a lover
She is me, where I begin.

Kundalini Fire

Silken trench, the tides have turned
kundalini lovers burn

Stargazing beyond mesmerised eyes
I see the gentleness that hides

Armour spilled across the floor
entwined our souls, I'll caress in awe

Now come.

Lay with me.

Let me lather you in a drenching.

Buzzing swirls of a love-hive
my delight, it comes alive

Please stay.

Dance with me.

Slowly enter, and I will surrender.

Claim me but do not cage me
like a wish upon a star, adore me from afar

Too fickle is our pride
heart space open, get ready to fly

Unravel my key for a place that hides
melting together two lovers' skies.

Bridging to an End

This idle thought is all-consuming
be that it may, I relinquish

Lustful dreams keeping claim
'to and fro' no longer appease

Anchor steady, my love
cease trade of eye for an eye

A little timid in my wild
softening to land

Great garden beds of slumber, must there be a sunrise?

I find glorious rapture in a knowing.

Passing Sorrow

I close my eyes to envision the skin lands my heart calls home.

Searching earthly scapes. Amongst the peaking pinnacles of Macedon rock, I gently puncture a rolling and clouded skyline.

Yet below the blue of heaven, there is a lingering mist. It settles in the valley.

Here I am.

My heart lies here.

In winter damp lands of Lyonville. But do not fear.

I feel your warmth flicker through my fragile glass.

I see you.

Peeking into this wooden shelter that houses my cubs. Can you feel my gentle radiance? A glow of puppy paws and tender hearts.

It envelops me. I feel it all around as your cool hands soothe my sorrow.

I rest now, knowing I am loved.

My heart will stay here.

Kate Hamilton

To my Husband

Dear Mike,

As a little girl, my thoughts on getting married and having a partner always centred around being a mother. That was always the priority. Then, as I got older, the idea and desire to find a nice man to settle down and have a family with dominated my thoughts. Unfortunately, finding the right man wasn't as easy as I thought it would be. I lacked self-esteem and didn't believe I was worthy, so I'm sure you can imagine the calibre of men I attracted wasn't ideal and when a man of substance came along, I'd inevitably find a way to sabotage the situation. In hindsight, I now believe that this was all the universe's way of ensuring I found my way to you and didn't get distracted.

When I found myself at the ripe old age of twenty-seven, I was already planning how to embark on parenthood as a singleton because, you know, the naïve twenty-something girl I was, believed there was no way I'd meet a man now I was getting close to my thirties. Now, as I approach my forties, I see how silly this was.

One night at a friend's wedding, there you were—tall, dark, handsome, funny, and had eyes for me. My previous bad habits surfaced, and it looked like I would sabotage a good thing again. But I was so unbelievably fed up with being stuffed around by men that I ignored all those instincts and went on a date with you.

From the first moment, I knew you were my guy. I laid it all out on the table, telling you I was done mucking around, and I was looking to settle down, and that marriage and babies were a must. We all know that this is #desperate behaviour for a first date, but my gamble paid off. We were on the exact same page. Phew!

Finally, I had found my other half, the person I knew I was supposed to meet and embark on my dream life with. I knew I'd found something special in you, but I had no idea just how special and what the universe had in store for us.

Like every couple, we had plans and dreams to expand our family. Fast forward six years, and we had done it: a house, marriage, a beautiful daughter, and a baby boy on the way. I still remember and often think about the phone call when I received the results of my prenatal tests. Everything came back normal and healthy, and the baby was a boy. I remember calling you bursting with excitement and telling you to get your footballs and fishing rods ready because your son is on the way, and, well, life just couldn't be more perfect.

When planning and getting excited about our future, special needs parenting never entered our thought process. I mean, let's be real no-one ever thinks it's something they'll ever be faced with. Even when you're pregnant and getting all the scans to make sure everything is okay, you never truly think your child won't be born healthy. But our special relationship called for special circumstances, and we found out our son was one in a few million, literally.

Disability parenting is tough, and I can definitely see how it tears apart marriages and relationships. Having a son with complex medical needs that will never get to walk or talk or live an independent life is heartbreaking. The heartbreak literally takes your breath away. But eventually, you catch your breath and adjust to your new normal. I never anticipated spending anniversaries, Father's Days and birthdays in the children's hospital or having to build a team to help us raise this extra-special child, but none of that has stopped us from having a laugh and staying true to ourselves.

Watching you with your children is my favourite thing. Witnessing you become this amazing, patient, hard-working father who will do anything for his son and his daughters inspires me daily. I'm proud of us, proud of our partnership and our ability to work in the trenches together. Through the sleepless nights, the hospital visits, the appointments, the illness, and all the scary unknowns. But most of all, I'm proud that we are still that same in-love couple, just older, stronger, and wiser, but still making plans and chasing our dreams.

Out of all the love stories out there, ours is my favourite … and it's worthy of the big screen.

All my love,

your wife, Kate.

Chantelle Dawn Skye

Poems for my Lover

Sweet Nectar of the Gods

I want to taste how you feel
As my mouth fills with words unsaid
It is you, I wish, who would fill it

With your breath, your tongue
Your undulating flesh
To dine on loves ambrosia

Swell and rise
Sweet nectar of the gods
I am here, I am complicit

With your touch, your lips
A cascade of sensations
Will be how the stars are lit

I want to meet you as we collide
Open, we entwine into raptures
As we worship the holy

Surge and flow
Sweet nectar of the gods
I am here, I am complicit

Honey in My Heart

Today I choose to soften
And open up for you
Feeling deep into this tenderness
So we can truly meet

I call you softly to me
So I can show you all
Of the poetry, you have inspired
Before we even met

Right now, I am sweet
With honey on my nipples
But how sweeter would I be
With you as the honey in my heart

Love, a Thousand Cuts

I am a galaxy
Shaped into the flesh of a woman
Exploding with stars from long-lost worlds

There are myths written in the curves of my bones
Carved in by my ancestors

Let them drip from my tongue
My voice reminding you of velvet
Feel them glide across your skin

I will stroke you like the ocean
In deep waves of emotion

Love is a thousand cuts to the soul
To which we intoxicatingly submit
Let me bathe yours with licks

Intimacy is the oxygen I seek
As I breathe myself into life

Seed of Me

I long for a rib cage that is willing to be cracked open
So that I may nestle in and call it my second home

A home in their heart space where the little seed of me is planted
And it shall grow into a garden of wild roses
Untamed but tended to by gentle, loving fingers

Knowing that this garden is a mirror
For what grows in the heart space of me

The Art of Love Self

Like a lantern beckoning through the darkness
I find the love I have been seeking
There it flows, cascading down my spine

Making its home nestled in my thighs
Worshipping the magic in my womb
Then it flows, ascending to the heart divine

I am the weaver, the warrior
The witch and the wisdom
Feeling the urge to no longer hide

But mostly, I am the woman, the human
The soul cradled in this body
Feeling the surge of me rise

And like a flame burning through the shadows
I find my own lover deep inside
Her love licks my lips the way I like

She makes her home nurtured in my unknown realms
Teasing out my own sweetness
And when we kiss, I taste my own delight

Aasta Ryan

Everlasting Light

Who would have thought that love and a relationship could be like this or feel like this?

Who would have thought that you could feel so safe, secure, loved and held and that it could be created and reciprocated?

Who knew the depths of the pleasure and the pain, the full body comfort and the agonising discomfort when you're triggered …

When we met, my world changed forever, not in a love-at-first-sight kind of way, but also kind of. Seeing your smile in the crowd and you seeing me, it was like the outside world became irrelevant. There was an energetic shift, and I knew I needed to know you. Your presence was so inviting, and your smile was so infectious. My heart, body and soul just wanted to be in your sphere. After some awkward interactions and three million questions, we connected, and when you kissed me, I couldn't speak!

What followed was a tumultuous journey of two people who hadn't known love and safety before learning how to create that with each other. It was intense! My heart and soul knew I needed you for the next phase of my healing and my life's journey. Right from the first time I met you, you felt like home to me. You felt safe—not in a familiar way, but in a way I'd never known before. It felt so intoxicating.

Over the years, we have unpacked our unconscious and conscious beliefs about love, relationships, and parenthood. It hasn't been easy, *but* it has been incredibly nourishing and rewarding. We have created such a united foundation and partnership based on openness, radical honesty, self-reflection and personal accountability with trust, loyalty and respect.

Now all of these sound very serious. To be honest, it kind of has been! We have always viewed it as pulling ourselves and our lives apart to build a new, solid foundation to move forward from, but growth, undoing, and rewiring can be painful. This is far from what we are sold in movies and books, and often, we have questioned if we are doing it all wrong.

It's difficult to find people role-modelling the kind of relationship we have and are continuing to create, but my relationship with you is one of my biggest achievements. We have always navigated it by our *own* internal compass and not by anything or anyone external.

We've also had plenty of laughs and fun along the way. Being in a relationship with you has taught me to look to the everyday instead of just the grand gestures and events. Our son does the same thing as you, buys and picks me flowers. You tell me daily how special, beautiful and wonderful I am. You know and appreciate my gifts in our relationship, and in return, you know that yours are valued, too.

As a woman, I was never taught or told to learn to support a man emotionally. Having you trust me to hold you through your unfolding has been one of the greatest gifts and biggest teachers. Learning to be patient and what true togetherness and selflessness look and feel like.

I'm proud of what we have created and continue to create, and I'm proud to model an example of a healthy relationship to our children and others. Our relationship is perfectly imperfect and authentically ours.

Here's what love is to me:

Love is wanting the best for your partner, regardless of what that means for you.

Love is watching you father our son consciously.

Love is losing a baby and navigating it with such tenderness and togetherness that it feels impossible not to be together forever. To declare our love to the universe and decide to elope and get married in our backyard.

Love is teaching, allowing and encouraging each other to express all emotions safely in our home.

Love is falling in love repeatedly as we both constantly evolve into more aligned versions of ourselves.

Love is choosing to help and hold each other daily while we re-parent ourselves to show up more wholly for our kids and each other.

Love is looking into your eyes and feeling completely seen and loved—for all the magnificent *and* all the messy bits.

Love is learning to hold and love each other, a gift that we both honour regardless of how difficult the challenge we navigate is

Love is feeling the exhale of my body when we hold hands or as I curl up to fall asleep on your chest.

Love is being thanked every day for all my contributions as a mother.

Marie Czatyrko

Love at First Sight

In late 1985 we decided it was time to fly from Melbourne to Perth to start a new chapter in our life.

Daughter number one, Bianca, is a four-and-a-half. Blind and Sassy! My niece was born, and I'm aunty and would be godmother. I'm looking after my younger sister, Gina's newborn, while she has some medical procedures done. I'm staying with her husband, Tony, and my cheeky four-year-old nephew, Louis. I had come out of an abusive relationship, so a change was best for my daughter and me. I would never ever be in the situation I was in with Bianca's biological father.

I met a wonderful lady, Judy, who was blind and had a vision-impaired daughter. We got on like a house on fire. She taught me the meaning of independence for vision-impaired children and adults. Through this time, I manifested a man who'd appreciate me for me and accept my daughter into his life without all the abuse.

On March 8, 1986, love at first sight happened. I was at a wedding the night before and caught the bouquet. Who knew that six months later, I'd be a bride?

My friend Judy and her partner, Peter, introduced me to Chris. We went down to the river on their boat for a picnic. There, Chris said he fell in love with me at first sight. He proposed to me three days later.

I said to Chris that I was a package deal. My daughter needs to like you. A big responsibility because I wasn't only a parent, but my daughter was blind.

When I manifested for this man, I wrote in journals. I think that after thirty-five years of marriage, I knew in my soul who I was looking for. Here goes.

Caress, Caressed hold me tight, for I am day, and you are night
Shatter, Shattered a million pieces, broken, torn, forever lost, I hear
the cry cold as frost.
Melt, Melted the blood that boils, metal taste of iron and stone. It
holds a love that needs no toil.
Release, released from the bond of wife, to share the space of freedom
of life.
Forever or never, the gift of time we share, what is yours is mine.
Soul, Souls, separate yet together, our story written here as is from
heaven.
Love, Loved, I feel it still entwined together like fire and steel.

So much heartache and love can come from living and learning about what the heart wants.

We know that logic does not reason with emotions. This makes it difficult to negotiate with yourself about decision-making. As a twenty-six-year-old, I'd lived to experience total heartbreak and abandonment. I became a mother to a child with a disability, which came with its own responsibilities that I couldn't share with a partner or husband. Yet I found it in my heart to give Chris a chance. A chance to see all the compassion, understanding and knowledge of truth in his heart. Chris and I could build and share a life and educate our daughter together.

The family unit became an extended family as European

backgrounds blended into one. We shared values and the meaning of togetherness with respect for each other.

Here I am thirty-five years later, still in love with my husband, who fulfils my every need. We are now in our twilight years and enjoying life to the fullest. We still love to go on holiday, but we're creatures of habit—we like going to our timeshare by the sea. Let's see what brings us joy from now, love.

Together forever. I Love you, Chris.

Love, Marie.

Enisa Cuturich

Divine Intervention

Dominik Sonderegger,

Your name still gives me all the lady tingles.

Our story is one that I will never tire of telling. It's one of those stories of two people meeting at the wrong time, then the universe working her magic with a little thing called divine intervention.

It's also an incredible reminder that we truly were meant to be.

Let's go back to when we officially first met, the moment when I experienced my first overpowering dose of lust. You sat across from me with your girlfriend sitting on your lap, and I completely lost control.

My eyes lit up like I'd just been given my first meal in years, my entire body sinking as my jaw dropped and I licked my lips. You caught me staring, and we both laughed. Then, you gave me this look, and I just thought, yep! I am in massive trouble!

I asked about you that day with everyone's response was the same, 'Stay Away!' which only made me want you more, and in true Enisa style, I thought, challenge accepted.

You quickly became my drug of choice, the only man who turned me into a little girl. Who made it safe for me just to be me and, let's be honest, could give me all the feels by just hearing your name.

That day was the start of years of sneaking into my window through the balcony, secret nights out, deep and meaningful conversations, and an undeniable connection.

But it was when we were twenty-two that we started to manifest our now life. It blows my mind how we talked in detail about running away together to an island and living out the rest of our years so that we could be together.

Our love was forbidden, but it was fun and exciting. The thrill of the sneak around and even the playfulness of both of us pretending like we didn't feel as deeply as we did.

We would vacation together in between the off seasons of our toxic love stories that we both lived, where we could once again fantasise about writing a love story that was destined to have a happily ever after.

I fell in love with you when our vacation was extended. That three months where you just held me amid the chaos I was going through. You reminded me of my worth, and you made sure that I was smiling from a place of genuine joy. You made me feel safe.

We had every reason under the sun not to be together, which seemed so real and big. But I look back now with my mature eyes, realising that none of it mattered.

Years went by, with a few sneaky conversations here and there. Messages of I miss you, and I'm thinking of you until we finally thought, what the fuck are we doing?!

It was time just to move on.

After five years of no contact, a drunk night out, and hearing the news that you were single, I added you on social media. Waking up in the morning regretting my decision, I cancelled the request, but you'd seen it.

Welcome Divine Intervention.

We organised to meet on a Friday, which was fast approaching, and in typical Enisa fashion, I freaked out. After one of the most chaotic days of my life and having no choice but to walk my angry, over-whelmed ass home from the middle of nowhere, I was going to cancel. I thought I don't need the drama! I am so different blah blah blah.

The ruminating about you and how I was making a bad decision didn't stop until I made a wrong turn down a random street … and there you were, getting out of your car.

And there I was once again, losing complete control like it was the first time I'd seen you.

Both of us shouted, 'WHAT THE FUCK?!' As you ran to me to hug me, kissing me while I was being taken back in time by the smell of you.

Overwhelmed AF, unable to stop smiling, I walked away from you and said, 'See you Friday.'

Looking at my phone to see it was 1:11 pm.

I wrote this on that day.

'The chapters we published in the past trigger my paralysing fear of picking up the pen of the present to discover the unwritten end of our story.'

You walked through my front door on September 4, 2020. Five days later, you told me you had put a baby in me. Then, on September 29, we found out you actually did. Ha-ha! Without a second thought, you told me you were all in, that you wanted forever.

Now we are living the life we always talked about, just You, Me and Baby Luka living on an island. I will be forever grateful that I picked up the pen to continue writing about our happily ever after.

I love you.

Laura Elizabeth

For Lovers

Milk Blood Cum

The three-course meal.
All of me
Bare
Vulnerable and open.

Stripped of my uncertainty, you showed me the key to unlocking my
power and assisted my process of reclaiming my wild woman.
Fiercely gazing upon my soul.
Your hands, your mouth and your words affirmed how much you
adored my body, my curves.
The way my breasts fall to the side as I lay there.
My legs open, and you drank from me.
Bathing in my sacred blood, drowning in a tsunami of my pleasure.
Oceans.

Painting our bodies in ceremony as you continued to devour me like I
was the centre of a pagan worship ritual, the centre of the universe.
Speaking in tongues.

How could I not have wanted more?

I learned so much through our dance.
Radical acceptance of myself and my body.
My hunger for pleasure, for exploration … for more!

I remembered all the things I had once loved and forgotten. Things I felt ashamed of, things that were forbidden.
With that key, with our dance, I remembered. I had permission to accept, enjoy and love them again.

I am grateful for your presence, even during your own dark winter of unravelling.
Even when you didn't feel safe, I did!
Even when you were risking all that you believed to be true.

Just one More Taste

Just one more taste!

She begged as the sweet nectar
glistened upon her tongue.
Forbidden, sexy, playfulness,
with the supportive hand
and enthusiastic voyeurism
of her beloved.

A delicacy!

A delicious addition
to an already wild
and full belly of love
in exploration,
of deeply courageous lusting.

A journey to love and know love
beyond that which our limited perception had allowed.
A longing to connect,
to unravel old paradigms
and shift awareness from gender to fluid.

From shame to pleasure.
Absolute.

Melting into You

I want to be soaked in the juices of our love.
Gasping for air as the waves flow over,
in and through the deepest parts of me.

Surrendering over and over
to meet myself
where life begins and ends,
with you as my witness.
Opening up to a million potentials
as we ride through time and space,
holding on tightly
in fear of escaping our bodies completely.

I want the smell of you
melted into my skin,
and the taste of me on your breath
as we take a moment
to rest between tides.

Janice Cooper

A Lifetime of Love

Dear Ian,

When I considered contributing to this chapter, my main concern was how I would condense our forty-two-year relationship into approximately 800 words. However, once the thought process began, I realised that it's more about what has led to you still being the most important person in my life.

We met in 1980 when I was fourteen, and you were sixteen. You have been my only lover, and I feel lucky to have been able to find my life partner at such a young age, creating a life with you I instinctively knew would work out.

After we met, we got to know each other over the next few years, and we fell into the comfortable feeling of being a couple.

We married in 1984, had our daughter in 1987, and completed our little family with a son in 1991. The memories we have created over the years are the most precious possessions we have, and I thank you for being the strong and supportive man I have needed many times throughout my life and for being the best father for our children.

We have a partnership that is rare by today's standards. I am always so proud to call you my husband. Your strong values and integrity make you so easy to trust, and you are always there for me, offering practical solutions when I am caught up in the emotional stresses of life.

Like all married couples, life hasn't always been easy, and we have had our share of sadness and financially tough times, but you have always been able to find a way to overcome any problems. You have taken the lead and shouldered the burdens when they have arisen. You are emotionally strong and extremely methodical, which is the complete opposite of me. As the saying goes, 'Opposites attract.'

As we all know, nobody is perfect, and neither is any relationship. There are obviously times when we have disagreed over various topics and circumstances. That is human nature. We have always managed to work out our differences without too much drama because of our mutual respect. Our relationship has certainly required the investment of a lot of work and time by both of us. We move together as the surrounding circumstances change. We grow older and learn to adjust to the changes in our lives and our individual personalities. Everyone evolves differently, and we have been lucky to stay together during our personal evolutionary process.

We have lived a full life, created two of the most wonderful children, and continue to evolve and grow throughout the many different chapters of our lives with a togetherness that feels stronger as the years go by.

We took a leap of faith when we emigrated to Australia in 1991 with our young family, and that was a testament to your desire to provide us all with a better life filled with opportunities that we could never have achieved in the UK. I trusted in you completely, and you provided us with a new life we have embraced wholeheartedly.

We have been together throughout many life changes. First, beginning our lives together, having our children and raising them, then letting them go to live their own lives independent of us, and throughout it all, you have been there.

Your humour is second to none, and you make me laugh at some point almost every day. When friends ask me if you're always joking around, I have to answer yes. I think it's one of the most endearing things about you. You never take yourself or life too seriously. I love the way you can diffuse an awkward situation with a quick-witted line and a bit of sarcasm thrown in for good measure.

I have come to realise, whilst writing this chapter, that our relationship over the past forty-two years has been filled with many small everyday acts which are too many to mention, and this is what makes our bond so strong and unwavering. You will always have my back because I trust you one hundred per cent. I can absolutely be myself when I'm with you, and you can make me feel safe and loved without having to say a word.

We are blessed to have found each other in this world, and I would change nothing. I have no regrets. I would choose the same life with you again and again. The good and the not-so-good times, and the memories made, are what have made our relationship the precious gift it is today. You have given me a lifetime of love, and I hope you know how much you are loved in return.

My love for you is forever.

Thank you for choosing me!

Jade Bell

The Lover

I see you there,
the way you stare.
Blue eyes search, unseeing,
lost in a moment of being.

We break away,
hope for a different day
Is there love there, lover?
Is it love like no other?

When we touch, how does it feel?
Is there longing there still?
Sometimes I wish we'd never met.
This flailing, twisting, torment,
for you to be the lover.

Fiona Cartledge

Always and Forever

We've met a thousand times or more. It has brought us to where it is so very raw! This rawness, it's painful, bringing up all that reminds us of how we've been hurt before. Better than that, though, is how completely perfect it feels. We see how much we've grown together and what and who we have created together. It's us, you and me, and nowhere else is where I'd rather be.

To see how in love we are after nineteen years together is something I treasure, and I am so deeply proud of us. We both know it hasn't been easy. We've had our share of challenges, and our stumbles on the road. Hey, we even thought we were too different and were so close to accepting that our time may have expired.

But …

We carried on. Walked through the flames. We walked the dark, dark road and finally, we are both in the light, shining bright, seeing our beauty, uniqueness and cheekiness and that it was always supposed to be this way. Maybe we took a little longer, and maybe we held onto things for too long. Maybe we carried with us the hurts of the past, past relationships, and didn't know it was us in the way of becoming this perfectly imperfect couple who deeply loves one another, including and accepting of all our madness, our imperfections and our some-times overly needy ways.

You're the one I wished for, you're the one I did the work for, and you're the one I want to be more confident for.

I believe in it working because you do. I want you to know that between all the frustration, ups and downs, and the sometimes mundane ways life can be a lot, it's worth it because of that great, amazing man that you are, that you've never not loved me, you chose me and only me, and It's you who I choose to spend the rest of my life with. Who could not love you, my man of steel?

More than those gorgeous green eyes and that perfect human suit you wear is the vulnerable side you've shown. That part of you that's only been shared with me, and I'll never make you regret it.

That heart of yours is pure, and it's a match for my pure love.

Grow with me
Glow with me
And make love to me forever
My Lover …

Let's celebrate ourselves. Let's celebrate you and me, we don't need a crowd, a cake or presents!

Just our smiles, our embrace, and both of our presence.

Let's celebrate being alive and feeling well.

We are worth celebrating!

If we just choose to step back and observe, to respond rather than react, to put our energy into understanding, acceptance, in trusting the unfolding and flow of life. If we spoke the truth from our hearts, not our heads …

To see the beauty and growth and rise above the challenges we face, making the best of a situation and taking breaks to let our best self-step in. Observing from a perspective higher than you and I and doing our best to embody that without needing it to be perfect, just better than before. Then slowly but surely, we will be guided peacefully on our paths carrying compassion, love and belief in ourselves and each other.

My heart loves your heart, and that's the path I'll keep returning to …

Me to you!
Forever and Always!
We've got this!
I'll be yours, and you'll be mine.

The feeling from a lover can also be like the emotions felt by certain energies and places. Being in a place of love, doing what you love, and absorbing that energy.

The way you feel about the ocean, how it listens, holds space, cleanses and calms.

It has no judgement, just pure unconditional love!

It's actually a vibrantly uplifting, pure heart and soul connection to have a feeling of home and pure bliss! Heaven on Earth for even just a few moments.

Filling every cell of your being with pure eternal love.

The most natural and beautiful love.

We can carry it with us and return to it whenever we choose, like a bird to a nest.

Love, Fiona.

A Letter to My Lover

Letters to my *Lover*

Letters to my *Lover*